# SQUEAK-A-LOT

*For Peter*
M.W.

*For Jane*
V.M.

Text copyright © 1991 by Martin Waddell
Illustrations copyright © 1991 by Virginia Miller
First published in Great Britain in 1991 by Walker Books Ltd.
First published in the United States in 1991 by Greenwillow Books
All rights reserved. No part of this book may be reproduced or utilized
in any form or by any means, electronic or mechanical, including
photocopying, recording, or by any information storage and retrieval
system, without permission in writing from the Publisher,
Greenwillow Books, a division of William Morrow & Company, Inc.,
105 Madison Avenue, New York, NY 10016.
Printed in Hong Kong by South China Printing Company (1988) Ltd.
First American Edition   10 9 8 7 6 5 4 3 2 1

Library of Congress Cataloging-in-Publication Data
Waddell, Martin.
Squeak-a-lot/written by Martin Waddell;
pictures by Virginia Miller.
p.   cm.
Summary: A mouse's search for someone with whom he
can play introduces him to a variety of animal sounds,
not all of which suit him very well.
ISBN 0-688-10244-1.   ISBN 0-688-10245-X (lib. bdg.)
[1. Animal sounds—Fiction.   2. Mice—Fiction.]
I. Miller, Virginia, ill.   II. Title.
PZ7.W1137Sq   1991   [E]—dc20
90-3568   CIP   AC

# SQUEAK-A-LOT

Written by
**Martin Waddell**

Illustrated by
**Virginia Miller**

Greenwillow Books, New York

In an old old house lived a small small mouse
who had no one to play with.

So the small small mouse went out of the house
to find a friend to play with.

And he found
**a bee.**

"Can I play with you?"
the mouse asked the bee.
"Of course," said the bee.
"What will we play?"
asked the mouse.
"We'll play Buzz-a-lot,"
said the bee.

BUZZ BUZZ BUZZ BUZZ BUZZ!
But the mouse didn't like it a lot.
So he went to find a better friend to play with.

And he found
**a dog.**

"Can I play with you?"
the mouse asked the dog.
"Of course," said the dog.
"What will we play?"
asked the mouse.
"We'll play Woof-a-lot,"
said the dog.

WOOF WOOF WOOF WOOF!
But the mouse didn't like it a lot.
So he went to find a better friend to play with.

And he found
**a chicken.**

"Can I play with you?"
the mouse asked the
chicken.
"Of course," said the
chicken.
"What will we play?"
asked the mouse.
"We'll play Cluck-a-lot,"
said the chicken.

CLUCK CLUCK CLUCK CLUCK!
But the mouse didn't like it a lot.
So he went to find a better friend to play with.

And he found a cat

"Can I play with you?"
the mouse asked the cat. And . . .

WHAM! BAM! SCRAM!
The mouse didn't like it a lot.

So he ran away through the long long grass
playing Squeak-a-lot all by himself.
SQUEAK SQUEAK SQUEAK SQUEAK!

SQUEAK! Some mice found the mouse.
"Can we play with you?" the mice asked the mouse.
"Of course," said the mouse.
"What will we play?" asked the mice.

"Buzz-a-lot!" said the mouse. BUZZ BUZZ BUZZ BUZZ BUZZ BUZZ BUZZ! And all of them liked it a lot.

"Woof-a-lot!" said the mouse. WOOF WOOF WOOF WOOF WOOF WOOF! And all of them liked it a lot.

"Cluck-a-lot!" said the mouse. CLUCK CLUCK CLUCK CLUCK CLUCK! And all of them liked it a lot.

"WHAM! BAM! SCRAM!" said the mouse.

SQUEAK SQUEAK SQUEAK SQUEAK!
The mouse chased the mice through the

long long grass back home to the old old house.
And together they played . . .

Sleep-a-lot.